OTHER REALMS
BREWPUB

by

Orion T. Hunter and Kyros Amphiptere

Copyright © 2019

Tesham Guild Publishing

All rights reserved.

ISBN: 978-0-9962665-4-3

THE NIGHT THE LIGHTS WENT OUT IN KANSAS

The Other Realms Brewpub, ORB to the regulars, was abuzz, full of its usual magical crowd. In one corner, a group of gnomes celebrated their soccer victory. By the bar, a coven of witches hunched over their cell phones, cackling about some new features that would make online casting spells easier.

Fergus Cassidy, fresh from guarding his family's pot of gold, had barely closed the glass door against the chill night air when the power went out. He pulled out his cell phone, intending to use its flashlight.

He tapped the screen.

Nothing happened.

Scowling, he tapped the screen a second time.

It was dead.

In the dark across the room, his friend Angelica shook her wings. Sparkling fairy dust drifted from them, providing enough dim light for him to make his way to her table. He sat down just in time to hear Dworkin say the final words to a spell. A fireball hurtled from the man's outstretched hand into the cold fireplace. The wood caught, brightening the pub enough so that Fergus could see the rest of the bar.

"Watch it, wizard," he shouted, patting down the singed edges of his beard. "Any idea what caused this?"

"Power outage?" Dworkin shrugged. "Maybe Dagan turned on too many gadgets in the kitchen?"

The banshee bartender, Morgan O'Grady, popped up from behind the bar.

"Nope. Dagan's in the dark, too." She poured a stein of beer, brought it over, and set it down in front of Dworkin. "Maybe someone hit a pole and blew a transformer?"

Angelica shook her head and gestured toward the windows. "Hunh-uh. Look outside. No lights anywhere." She took out her ancient flip phone, mashing buttons to no avail. "Nothing electrical seems to be working."

Celeste, one of the witches at the end of the bar, stood up. "Marta just did a scrying. Someone detonated an EMP bomb over Iowa. The whole country's lost power."

The entire room groaned.

"Oh, *HELL* no! I am *not* living without my cell phone," someone shouted.

Sitting by the fireplace and clutching his laptop to his chest, the genie, Robin, let out a screeching wail. "Or my World of Warcraft!"

"Eh, who cares?" Muttered, Tiatha, the ancient elf, from a table by the door. "Maybe we'll go back to the good ole days," she gestured to include the whole room, "before all this damn technology took over."

Fear spread across Fergus' face. "Wait, does that mean no more Starbucks? I can't function without my morning coffee."

Patting him on the back, Angelica said, "If you didn't drink so much ale every night, Fergus, maybe you wouldn't *need* coffee every morning."

"Details, details," Fergus spat back. Looking around at the gathered magical creatures in the ORB, he crossed his arms and growled, "What are *we* going to do about this?"

"Us?" the room responded in unison.

"Who else? The humans? Without technology, they're

pretty much useless. We've at least got our magic to fall back on."

Marta jumped to her feet. "We *could* do it," the witch said, stroking her long chin. "But we'd have to be quick. Resetting a major event like this means our window of magical elasticity runs out...," she looked to her coven mates for confirmation, "at midnight tomorrow night."

Fergus looked around the pub, meeting the eyes of every creature.

"I'm a fourth generation Leprechaun-American. This is my country too. We gotta help the humans. But we," he gestured to include everyone there, "can't do it all by our lonesome. We need to get the *entire* magical community to help. We gotta reach out to all our brothers and sisters across the country."

"So, Fergus, what's next? How do we organize this...this reset?" Angelica asked, her eagerness making her wings spread fairy dust, which lit up her beautiful face.

Fergus turned to Marta. "Can you get word to the other covens around the country...."

It was nearly sunset the next day, and the ORB was packed.

Creatures from all over the Midwest had descended upon the bar to take part in the upcoming magical event. The room glowed softly, lit by the candles and lanterns Morgan and Dagan had placed throughout the room.

Fergus rose, clapping his hands for attention.

"We've just received word from the East Coast. The working is well underway. The black hour is upon us; it's time for *us* to join in. Get ready."

As though on the wind, the sound of millions of voices raised in song drifted through the room.

Robin's eyes bugged out of his head. "It's a song from the heart, like something woven of everyone's hopes and dreams," the genie whispered to Angelica. "I've never seen anything like this, not in all the centuries I've been alive."

"I know." Her face shone. "It's wondrous!"

Around them, the patrons of the ORB began softly, their varied faces illuminated by the lantern and candlelight, each creature joining his or her voice to those of the whole country.

As the last of the West Coast passed into twilight and the entire nation had joined in—something shifted.

From the darkness came a light, exploding across the country like a strange new sun.

Everyone rushed to the windows.

Nothing was visible except a brilliant white light.

As it dimmed and the world returned, Angelica pointed. "Look! They're on! The street lamps are coming back on."

Everyone cheered their spell's success.

Through the din, Fergus' heard his cell phone ring.

Snatching the device from his pocket, he answered cheerily, "Hello?"

"Hello, the purpose of this call is to collect on a debt. This call may be monitored for training purposes...."

Fergus rolled his eyes and stabbed the disconnect button.

Raising his hand, he called across the bar, "Morgan, I need a drink. Now!"

The leprechaun lowered his head to the table and muttered, "Maybe we should have left well enough alone."

WORKING THE BUGS OUT

"Hey, Morgan, can we get another round of IPAs over here?" Dworkin called across the Other Realms Brewpub.

"You want the same one as last time, or something different?" the banshee bartender yelled back.

The mage perused the sign hanging over the bar listing the massive selection of drinks and concoctions available. "Too many choices!" he barked. "Surprise me."

Dworkin resumed his conversation with his fellow mage, Winifred. When Morgan dropped the two tankards of India Pale Ale on their table, the pair rocked back in their seats.

"Damn, woman," Winifred snarled, bending to pick her knitting up from the floor. "You shouldn't sneak up on a wizard like that. It might end badly for you."

The banshee chuckled and arched an eyebrow at the mage. "I've served demons, angels, and things that go bump in the night. I'm not scared of a..." She looked Winifred up and down. "barely hundred year old mage."

Dworkin rushed in before things got out of hand. "Uh, thanks, Morgan," he said, gruffly. "Put it on my tab."

The banshee chuckled. "Already done. And I included your favorite power boost additive, since you mentioned you have a long night of spellcasting ahead."

Dworkin took a sip of the beer and sighed happily. "Just what I needed. Thanks, Morgan."

Winifred pointed one of her knitting needles towards the bar. "I see you finally got a new guy to clean up the place. Glad Dagan's letting you off the hook a bit. You were working yourself to *death's door*, dearie."

Morgan rolled her eyes at the mage's horrible joke.

"Yeah, he's great. His name's Kizumono. He's an akaname, so he keeps the place spotless."

Dworkin turned to look at the subject of their conversation.

"A Japanese filth licker?" He blinked in surprise. "I've never seen one in person, only heard about them." He leaned toward her and lowered his voice. "Is it true what they say? Do they lick *everything* clean?"

Morgan made a face. "Yes, he licks the entire *bathroom* clean." She shuddered. "All of it. And I've seen the messes some of you make in there. I don't even want to go in there half the time, let alone clean it. We're really lucky to have him."

As if on cue, Fergus fell off his barstool and tossed his magically-undelicious cookies all over the floor.

Kizumono bolted across the barroom, his too-long tongue already trailing out the side of his mouth. By the time the inebriated leprechaun had managed to clamber back up onto his stool, there was no evidence that anything untoward had even happened.

"Well...," Dworkin gulped, "that was disturbing."

Morgan smiled sweetly. "And that's exactly why I asked Dagan to hire him. I told the boss if I had to clean up after one more botched spell or drunken bar fight, I'd quit."

Winifred cackled. "At least he's fast. That could have been...olfactorily unpleasant. I wouldn't want that smell to get into my knitting...."

Just then, the TV screen over the bar went to commercial, the volume blasting out at five times its previous level.

WIZARD ENTERPRISES WANTS YOU TO THINK THEIR NEW

DOOR-TO-DOOR PORTAL, THE D2D, IS A SAFE TRANSPORTATION DEVICE, BUT HOW CAN WE BE SURE THAT IT WON'T FAIL ONE DAY AND SEND YOU TO THE MOON INSTEAD?

The TV showed a man in a three piece suit standing on the surface of the moon, gasping for air.

WHAT IF SOMEONE ELSE IS ALREADY STANDING WHERE YOU ARE SUPPOSED TO APPEAR? WHAT HAPPENS THEN?

An image of two people superimposed with blood everywhere filled the screen in vivid color, looking for all the world like something from a horror movie.

FREE THINKING PEOPLE WANT ANSWERS TO THESE QUESTIONS! CALL OR WRITE YOUR CONGRESSMAN TODAY AND TELL THEM TO LOOK INTO THESE SHADY WIZARDS BEFORE SOMEONE GETS HURT. Tiny letters and a scroll covered with a red international symbol for 'NO' filled the screen. PAID FOR BY REMIT, RESIST EXTRANEOUS MAGIC IN TRANSPORTATION.

The TV returned to 'On a Wing and a Tail', a soap opera about a mermaid who falls in love with a gryphon.

Dworkin thumped the table. "Damned humans! Always afraid of every new thing. I bet that group is funded by the auto and airline industries. They know we'll make them obsolete."

"Besides, we've already thought of all those things," Winifred said, putting down her knitting. "It's perfectly safe to use. That's all just scare tactics."

Morgan glanced back and forth between the two mages. "So, it's been thoroughly tested then?"

Looking exasperated, Dworkin nearly shouted, "Of course." He paused for a moment, visibly calming himself. "Well, maybe a few of the initial test subjects went missing in action, but we've worked all the bugs out now."

Morgan smiled and started back toward the bar. A huge house fly buzzed around her and landed on the mages' table.

Spinning, Morgan attempted to squash the bug.

"STOP!!"

Morgan froze in mid-swat.

The fly scuttled across the table, stopping in front of

Dworkin. The bug waved its tiny legs. "Dworkin, it's me, Baldon. I didn't disappear. I accidentally merged with a house fly that was at the landing site. I've been trying to find someone to tell but everyone keeps trying to kill me! You have to tell the council there is a major flaw with the device before it goes public."

Winifred blanched. "We've got to report this. People could get hurt." She looked at Baldon. "And we've got to get you changed back."

"Here. Me clean. Kill bug."

Kizumono's long tongue slid across the table, sweeping their leftover snacks away.

And Baldon the fly as well.

"Wait...."

"Noooo...."

"Oh, dear...."

All three gaped at the akaname's red back as he lumbered away.

After several moments of silence, Dworkin glared at Morgan and Winifred.

"We did *not* just see a talking fly." He raised a menacing eyebrow. "I didn't and neither did either of you?"

Winifred nodded knowingly. "Nope. Didn't see a thing."

Morgan raised a finger. "But...."

Lightning danced across both mages' hands.

The banshee eyed them, obviously assessing the threat. After a moment, she shrugged. "It's not worth the scorch marks I'd get on my clothes."

As she headed back to the bar, Morgan took out her phone. "Siri, sell all my stock in Wizard Enterprises and..." The banshee paused to toss a dirty look at the mages over her shoulder. "remind me to get a car."

HOW IT ALL BEGAN

Morgan glanced around the pub as she placed another beer stein in the dishwasher. The bar's patrons sat huddled around their tables, waiting for the storm to pass so they could go home. Kizumono finished wiping down a table vacated by a group of water sprites, then joined her behind the bar.

"Wet ones go," he muttered. "Weather bad. Others afraid. Stay."

From the end of the bar, Fergus let out a laugh and gestured toward Kiz. "A real conver.... Hic! Conver...hic...sationalist, that one, eh?"

Morgan glared at the leprechaun and raised an eyebrow. "At least I can understand *him*." She grabbed the towel stuffed in the back pocket of her jeans and wiped away the condensation rings left by his beer. She sighed and placed yet another coaster in front of him. *Maybe this time he'll actually use it.* "Between how thick your damn accent gets and how badly you slur your words, even *I* can't understand you half the time."

"Bah! 'S not that bad!" he protested. "Errerybody unner-stands me. Right, Kiz, old boy?"

The akaname cocked his red, warty head at the short man. "Talk funny. Always drunk. Never tips."

Morgan covered her mouth to keep from laughing outright.

"Seems like Kiz knows you pretty well, Fergus."

The little man waved dismissively. "Who cares what you think." Chugging the last of his beer, he shook the stein at Morgan. "If ye'd stop making fun of a paying customer for a moment, love, I'd like another Dagan's Original Roscommon Bock."

"Coming right up, *sir*," she said with a half-salute. "We always take care of our *paying* customers." Baring all her teeth, she smiled as she set the cold brew in front of him. "And does that mean you plan to settle up your tab tonight? You owe for the last two months. Or," she said, saccharine dripping from her every word, "you could always switch to *iced tea*. It's much cheaper."

Fergus paused, the stein halfway to his mouth. "Now, now, lassie, let's not be hasty." He took a big gulp of his beer. Wiping the foam from his upper lip, he asked, "Soooo.... I've always wondered, how did you and Dagan meet, anyway? I mean, a pooka and a banshee running a bar? That sounds like the beginning of a bad joke."

Kiz leaned against the bar, nodding furiously. "Yes. Me want know."

Morgan chuckled. "You really want to hear about that?" When they both leaned closer, she shook her head. "Okay then." She tapped her finger to her lips. "It was...the late 1500s, I think. My family was on our annual pilgrimage to Newgrange when we stopped at an inn for the night." She rolled her eyes. "It turned out to be one Hell of a night...."

"Welcome to the Athlone Arms, ladies."

The dark skinned youth hurried to greet us, grabbing the horse's bridle as my mother dismounted.

"My, my, what a lovely mare this is," he said, stroking the horse's black neck. "We dinna get ones as fine as her very often." Then he noticed my aunts and I. "Please," he said, sweeping one arm toward the door, "all of you, come inside our fine establishment."

"I am Macha," my mother said. She gestured to my aunts who had come up to stand on either side of her. "These are my sisters,

Anand and Badb." She nodded toward the troop of children piling out of the back of the caravan that my cousin Flynn, the redcap, was driving. "And the rest of our brood. We require food and lodging for the eve."

The young man's eyes bugged out a bit at the number of us. "Then you have surely come to the right place." He fixed me with his gaze. "And who is the comely lass behind ye?"

A spark passed between us as my mother answered him. "Ah, that be my daughter, Morgan."

He held out his hand to me. "A pleasure, Morgan. My name is Dagan. My father, Cianán Quinn, owns this establishment."

I eyed his hand. *No one ever talks to me. They are usually too in awe of my mother and my aunts to even notice me. This boy...he is different.* I smiled and offered him my hand. He kissed it.

"Come, girls," mother said, grabbing my arm and hauling me through the door. "It is past time for a meal."

"So, why are you all on the road?" Dagan asked a few minutes later as he finished setting up the last table for us. Our party filled the large room, causing some of the locals to grumble about the crowded conditions.

"Pilgrimage," I answered. "To the temple at Newgrange. We go every year around this time." I slid my cloak off my shoulders and draped it over the chair in front of me.

"Those pretty blue feathers on your cloak? Are they kingfisher's?"

I laughed at his lucky guess. "Yes. The birds are the symbol of our house. They live by water, like my clan does. Galway by the Sea."

Dagan nodded, then excused himself. "I need to get more chairs from the shed. We seldom have this many guests all at once."

I made to follow him to continue our conversation, but he put out a hand to stop me.

"No, darlin'. You are a guest. My father would flay me if he caught me accepting help from you." The twinkle in his eyes made me laugh.

"Well, that's *almost* enough encouragement to make me carry all the chairs by myself. I have never seen anyone flayed before." Straining to contain my laughter, I continued, "Though my aunts say that it is truly a sight to behold."

His eyes widened. "Well, I hope you do not get a chance to see it here tonight!"

After all my relatives had seats, he returned, leaning against the wall next to me. "Newgrange? I heard it had long since been abandoned."

I sighed. "And it used to be so busy. When I was young, fifty priests and priestesses made it their home."

"Then why do you still go?"

I shrugged. "Tradition, I guess. Tradition is very important in my family." I chuckled. "My mother and aunts will probably still be going there when the world ends."

He nodded. "Now, *that,* I can understand. My da is like that too." He huffed a sigh. "I hope *I* never get so stuck in a rut like that."

"Oh, really? I bet you stay right here for the rest of your life," I teased. "You know you will end up just like him."

He shook his head violently. "Noooo, not me. I plan to open my own pub. In the Americas." His eyes twinkled. "I hear it is a harsh new land. Surely they will need a good pub to drink their problems away."

I laughed out loud, causing my mother at the next table to raise an eyebrow at me. Biting my lip, I looked down before I went on.

"You know, Mister Dagan Quinn? I like your idea. Maybe I could join you in that enterprise. I love my family and all, but they can be...difficult at times." I took a deep breath. "And I could use a fresh start too."

"Mavourneen!" My cousin Flynn tugged furiously at my tunic sleeve. I glared at him for using that childish nickname in front of Dagan. "You gotta see the carriage that just pulled up outside! It's beautiful. And the horses...."

That got both my and Dagan's attention.

We hurried outside. A coal black carriage with four inky black mares stood in the courtyard. The horses' blazing red eyes tracked Flynn warily as he reached up to stroke one of them. The horse threw its head back, snorting a stream of fire at him.

"By the Goddess!" Flynn cursed, stuffing singed fingers into his mouth.

"My horses are not for children, young man," said a crimson-clad gentleman. "I would not...further upset them, were I you."

Dagan recovered first. "Welcome to the Athlone Arms...." His voice trailed off when the stranger's gaze swept over us.

"Oh, and what have we here? A redcap, a pooka, and...." He tilted his head, narrowing his eyes at me. "Very interesting," he mused with a leering sort of a smile. "You are a banshee, but there is something...else about you. I cannot quite put my finger on it."

My mother chose that moment to come storming out of the pub. I closed my eyes and hid my face in my hands. "I gcuntais Dé!"

"Watch your language, girl!" she spat out, marching past me and right up to the man. Shaking a finger at him, she ordered, "You best not be bothering my daughter, demon."

His eyebrows rose as his gaze sharpened on me. "Macha's daughter?" He steepled his index fingers and tapped them on his lips. "So that is what is different about you, little one. You are not just a simple banshee. You are the daughter of an aspect of the Morrigan." He descended from the carriage. "Delightful! A baby goddess."

I snorted at that. "Me? I will *never* be a goddess. I am the youngest of twelve. The chance of my mother's mantle passing to me is beyond absurd."

Before I realized what he was doing, he took my hand and kissed it.

Two kisses in one day? Did mother put a glamour on me or something so that men would find me irresistible?

"You are lovely, child. Even if you never inherit your mother's title, you clearly have her fiery spirit." He gave me a devilish grin. "I like that in a potential mate."

My mother's eyes flashed in the twilight. Twin pools of fire flared at the stranger. She threw an arm between us, warning him, "Leave my daughter alone, Satan, or you will face my wrath."

I suddenly realized my aunts had come out of the inn and were flanking my mother and I. My auntie Badb even brandished her sickle, a wicked gleam in her eyes.

I put a hand on mother's arm, shaking my head. "Do not worry, mother. He is too boorish. I would never go with him!" I glared at the smiling demon. "Not in a thousand years."

That only made his grin broader. "We will see, my beauty. We will see."

Morgan was jolted out of her story by the simultaneous explosions of lightning and thunder.

Fergus jumped off his bar stool. "Ye Gods! Did tha' hit the building?"

"No, you're safe, little man," Satan said, dropping onto the bar stool next to Fergus. "For now."

Then, leaning in close to Morgan, he grinned broadly, his dark eyes glinting with humor. "It's been five hundred years, yet here I am, still trying to get that date."

Kiz shook his head. "Bathroom dirty. Me clean. *Now*." The akaname scurried away from the bar.

Fergus was looking everywhere but at Satan and I.

I closed my eyes and counted to ten. Then twenty. By one hundred, I could feel his gaze burning into me.

Taking a deep breath, I opened my eyes and gritted out, "No date! Not. In. A. *Thousand*. Years!"

LAST CALL

It was closing time at the Other Realms Brewpub.

"Last call was half an hour ago, everyone," Morgan called, coming around the end of the counter, a damp bar cloth in her hand. "Anyone who isn't out of here in five minutes risks incurring my wrath."

The minotaur snorted. "I'll leave," he growled, smoke billowing from his nostrils, "when I'm done with my beer."

Morgan's eyes narrowed. "Trust me. None of you wants to see an angry banshee."

The few remaining patrons made a swift exit. They'd all heard the story about the last time someone refused to leave.

Morgan smiled at the minotaur. "Looks like it's just me and you now, buddy." She inhaled sharply, preparing to scream.

The minotaur downed his beer, tossed some money on the table, and bolted out the door.

Exhaling, Morgan took a long look around. *They're all gone. Now I can relax.*

Her peace and quiet was abruptly shattered by a loud, resonant snore. Following the racket, she found Fergus, passed out drunk, under a table in the leprechaun's usual spot by the fireplace.

"Come on, Fergus," she said, shaking his shoulder. "We're

closed. Time for you to go home, boyo. You're drunk. Again."

"*Níl mé ar meisce[1],*" he complained. "Beshides, ish still errly."

"*Tá sé trí a chlog ar maidin[2].* Look, ya drunken gold-hoarder. I don't care where you go, you just can't stay here."

Grabbing her phone from her back pocket, she called the local cab company. "Hey, Danielle, I need a cab.... Uh huh, for Fergus.... Yes, again.... Thanks!"

"Ah, the devil take ye!" Fergus yelled, teetering toward the door.

She laughed. "Been there, done that. Your cab will be here any minute. Now git!"

Morgan shoved the diminutive leprechaun out into the parking lot and slammed the door.

"There. Finally! Alone at last."

Heading back to the bar, she noticed a lone shadowy figure sitting in the corner booth.

"Dammit," Morgan screamed. "I told you all to leave. Get out. This is *my* time now."

The black-cowled intruder rose and moved toward her.

A deep sonorous voice came from within the folds of its hood. "I've come for you."

She sniffed the air. Brimstone.

"Me?" Morgan chuckled. "Ah, it's not my time and you know it. Besides, you're in the business of collecting souls and we both know I don't have one."

The tall, cloaked demon shrugged. "Well, the leprechaun did ask me to...."

"Him?" she scoffed. "Since when do you listen to mortals?"

The dark figure chuckled. "Never! But since I hadn't seen you in a while, I thought I'd stop by anyway."

Reaching up and pulling his hood back, she smiled. "So, what've you been up to lately, Satan?"

"Same old, same old," he said dismissively as they moved to sit at the bar. "Do you have time to play a game with an old friend?"

"Of course. I've always got time to kick your ass."

"Well, you did beat me rather badly last time," he admitted. "Is it a banshee thing? Are they all as good as you are?"

She laughed. "No, only the ones from the lower east side of Galway." She raised an elegant eyebrow at him. "Same stakes as usual?"

He nodded. "Loser serves as a slave to the winner. For one week."

"Let's get down to business then," she said, a wicked smile dancing across her lips.

"My business is evil," he intoned, trying to keep a straight face.

"Mine's death, but let's just forget that for tonight and have a nice game, huh?"

"The usual?"

"Of course." She grabbed several items from under the counter, quickly setting up the game.

"I went first last time," he said, "so I guess it's your turn."

Morgan grabbed the bones lying on the bar and tossed them.

She counted off, "One, two, three, four, five, six, seven." She moved her shoe across the board and grabbed a card. "Take a ride on the Reading Railroad, if you pass GO...."

[1] I'm not that drunk.
[2] It's three in the morning.

FOOD OF THE GODS

It was unusually quiet in the Other Worlds Brewpub as Morgan made her way to the table where two preternaturally beautiful beings sat deep in conversation.

When the banshee placed the tray on their table, twin pairs of molten gold eyes beamed up at her.

"I brought you something to sample. Dagan's considering adding it to the regular menu," she said with a sly smile.

"Oh?" Hebe arched her perfect eyebrow at the bartender. "You know I love *anything* new."

"That's why I saved it for you and Ganymede. Have a taste and let me know what you think." Morgan set plates containing small square cakes in front of each of them. Stepping back, she crossed her arms—waiting.

Ganymede lifted the confection and took a cautious nibble. His eyes widened and his handsome face broke into a radiant smile.

"Wow! That's amazing! And such an interesting texture." He looked up at Morgan. "What is it?"

Hebe, in between bites, answered, "Don't you recognize it? It's ambrosia! Oooh, what a treat!"

Morgan smiled, then uncorked a bottle, filling two tankards. She handed one to each of the Olympians.

Hebe peered closely at her drink. Holding the glass up to the light, she marvelled, "It's plaid." She swirled the liquid. "And it stays that way. What *is* this?"

Morgan snickered. "Take a sip, then tell me what *you* think it is."

The immortals both took cautious sips of their colorful drinks.

Ganymede moaned in pleasure. "'Tis honey mead. I've never seen it's like outside Olympus itself." He paused a moment to consider his glass. "Though usually it's striped, not plaid."

The banshee refilled their tankards.

Hebe watched her closely. "By the Gods, it even pours plaid!" she exclaimed. "How did you come by this?"

Ganymede wiped the plaid froth from his lips. "Did Dagan learn how to make this? Is that why you're adding it to the menu?"

The banshee shrugged her pale shoulders, amusement playing across her face. "Trade secret."

Taking another huge gulp, Ganymede belched. "That is *the* best ambrosia and honey mead I've had in over a thousand years."

Hebe, mouth full of ambrosia, nodded vigorously while reaching for her tankard.

"Enjoy," Morgan said, turning back toward the bar. "Just flag down Kizumono if you want more."

As she entered the kitchen, Kiz came up behind her.

"Trade secret?" He pointed to the table where the two gods were scarfing down the small square cakes. Looking at her quizzically, he said, "Dagan no here. You make?"

Morgan chuckled, raising her hands. "Not me. I can't cook, I burn water." Morgan shook her head. "Besides, ambrosia and honey mead are *way* too much trouble to make from scratch."

Kizumono tilted his massive crimson head.

"Where come from?"

Smirking, Morgan reached under the counter and pulled out a shopping bag.

The akaname's eyebrows shot up. He glanced in the bag, his eyes going wide.

"If you tell anyone," the bartender said, pointing a finger at him, "you are so fired." She hooked her thumb, pointing at the two patrons. "Those two would freak out if they knew their *delicacies* came from a *grocery* store."

Kizumono pointed at the bag, sputtering, "Trader Joe's?"

Morgan shrugged. "Why are you so surprised? They carry all *kinds* of weird stuff."

NOT TODAY, SATAN

Maybe I should relocate to somewhere warmer, Morgan thought as she shivered, her breath pluming in the icy night air. *Nah, this place it too much fun. Where else could I associate with leprechauns, centaurs, vampires, and witches all in one place?*

The music in her headphones abruptly changed from sixties hard rock to nineties grunge. *Kurt Cobain,* she thought with pleasure. *Now* he *was a musician! I wonder where he ended up? Maybe I should ask Satan. He'd probably know.*

She closed the glass door of the Other Worlds Brewpub, then walked a few steps away before turning back. Pulling her phone from the skin-tight leather pants she wore, she watched the icon on the app change to locked as she heard the deadbolt slam into place.

I love this new gizmo Dagan installed. The doors automatically lock when I leave. No more bulky keyrings tearing up my pants. I could just kiss whoever invented this. She considered a moment. *Though not everyone would enjoy a kiss from a banshee.*

"Isn't it a little late to be out here all by your lonesome, babe?"

She pivoted slowly. Behind her, five hoodie-clad men stood in a semi-circle, penning her against the ORB's front door.

Tilting her head and smiling, she purred, "Guys, you really

don't wanna do this. I could literally kick your collective asses without breaking a sweat."

The tallest one, obviously the leader, barked a short laugh. "You might be able to take one or two of us, but there are three too many of us for you to handle." He pulled out a knife. "You need to be taught a lesson, bitch."

Morgan snorted. "Not today, Satan."

A handsome man in an expensively-tailored suit materialized beside her. "You rang? It's about time you got back to me," he said smoothly, a sparkle in his dark eyes. "You've been cancelling plans with me for weeks now. If it's something I said, just tell me." He crossed his arms, leaning back against the doorframe.

"I was just thinking about you. Do you know what ever happened to Kurt Cobain..."

"Who the hell is this guy?" the punk interrupted.

"Hell?" Satan smiled slyly. "How wonderfully ironic." He gestured toward the men. "Friends of yours?"

She shook her head.

"No, I think they plan to hurt me. Maybe even rape me."

He looked her up and down, appraising her leather pants, low-cut blouse, and leather jacket.

"Um, maybe they wouldn't bother you if you didn't dress like that. Not that I don't find your attire...stimulating."

Frowning, Morgan said, "Let me get this straight." She aimed a finger at him. "You're saying I should dress differently so that they won't try to rape me?"

Satan nodded.

"Soooo," Morgan drawled out, putting her hands on her hips, "you're saying you'd rather they try to rape someone else, then?"

Satan's perfect eyebrows shot up. "Ummmm...no. Uhhhh...I never really thought about it like that before."

Morgan nodded. "Of course you haven't." She rolled her eyes. "Typical man."

"Me?" His hand flew to the breast of his tailor-made suit. "A typical man? I take exception to that description."

She sighed. *Of course, everything's always about him.*

"Look. There will always be a woman who is less sober, less secure, walking in a darker part of town. She should be just a safe as I am."

"Enough of the chit-chat, whore," the leader of the gang broke in. "Your boyfriend ain't gonna save you."

Morgan looked sideways at Satan. "He is *so* not my boyfriend."

Satan looked down at himself. "Oh! They don't recognize me." Snapping his fingers, he transformed into his traditional Devil guise, complete with horns and pitchfork.

The gang leader backed up a step, looking back and forth between Morgan and Satan.

"Oh, no, my friend," Satan said, showing his teeth in a huge grin. "It's not me you need to worry about." He waved a red, gnarled hand toward Morgan. "She's your problem right now." His grin widened. "I'll get you eventually—maybe sooner if you don't survive this encounter." He shrugged. "Either way, you're mine."

All five gangbangers started backing away.

"Oh, don't run off," Morgan said, handing Satan her leather jacket and cracking her knuckles. "We're just getting started."

Grabbing the leader's hoodie, she yanked him off his feet. When the others came to his rescue, she dealt with them all quite handily.

"I do so love watching you work, my dear," Satan commented from the sidelines.

"Would you behave?" she said, delivering a solid punch to the last hoodlum still upright. The man spun in place before falling face first onto the asphalt.

Satan raised a hand in a gesture of surrender. "Far be it from me to interrupt your fun."

"Shut up or you're next!" she shouted, pointing a threatening finger at him.

"Oooh, sounds delicious," he said, shifting back into his normal appearance.

Giving her a lecherous smile, Satan stepped closer and helped her into her jacket. "Does this mean we're finally going on a date?"

She gave him a withering look and pretended to check her non-existent watch. "I said a thousand years. I *meant* a thousand years. Now, leave me alone."

Satan, with a pout, snapped his fingers and changed into a pirate.

As he faded out, he singsonged, "As you wiiiish...."

N.I.M.B.Y.

"Boss?"

Dagan jumped, upsetting a carafe of oil and nearly obliterating several platters of lunches ready to serve. Kizumono had climbed halfway through the serving window, his red, warty, frog-like face mere inches from Dagan's.

"What?!" the cook shouted.

Kiz vanished. The akaname's eyes slowly peeked back over the edge of the opening.

Damn. He's probably afraid I'll throw something at him. It's a good thing we rescued him from that hellhole he was in.

"Problem. Humans here. Suits. MegaBooze." The busboy jerked a thumb over his shoulder. "Want you."

Dagan rolled his eyes. Wiping his hands on his apron, he untied it and hurled it onto the counter. Storming out of the kitchen, he demanded, "Where are they?"

Kiz pointed a shaking hand toward the group of corporate drones huddled around one of the high tables near the front door. Morgan stood before them, arms crossed with a scowl on her face that would scare a demon.

As Dagan approached, he heard Morgan growl, "If you're not going to order anything, get out of my bar!"

"Fine!" the tallest one replied, looking down his nose at her.

"Get us four bottles of that amazing craft brew your boss makes."

Morgan raised an eyebrow. "Quinn's Original Roscommon Bock?"

"Sure an' ye be telling me what's this about then?" Dagan interrupted, his anger allowing his Irish brogue to emerge.

A pasty-faced man stepped forward, extending his hand. "Hello, sir. My name is Tab Harthan."

"Tabhartha?" Dagan asked, exchanging a humorous look with Morgan. *I figured the man would be a bit of a git, but I didn't expect his bloody name to be 'bastard' in the old language.* He chuckled at the thought.

The man shook his head, whipping out a business card and placing it in Dagan's hand. "No, no, it's Tab Har-*than*."

"You're from MegaBooze, aren't you?" Dagan's anger rose. "I *told* you I wasn't interested in selling my bar. Especially not to you misbegotten louts!"

He paused to collect himself.

Morgan grabbed his arm. "Why do they even want to buy a magical bar in the middle of Nowhere, Kansas?"

Dagan sniffed. "Hmph. For the secret of my special brew, of course. You know that any human we get in here can't get enough of it. I'm guessing word got back to these dolts."

The banshee made a face. "Figures."

"A' course I've turned them down. Repeatedly." He gestured toward the trio of suits. "They seem to think showing up here will change my mind."

The hairs on the back of his neck rose.

Glancing around, he saw the mage, Dworkin, waving his hands and preparing to cast a spell. Fergus, too, had risen and was advancing on the trio, the leprechaun's shillelagh raised menacingly. Dagan could feel the witches in the corner were up to something as well, but he was afraid to look.

Morgan followed his glance. Squaring her shoulders, she marched toward Fergus and Dworkin.

"If you know what's good for you, stay out of this!" When Dworkin didn't stop, Morgan pointed a finger at him. "Don't you dare!"

Snatching Fergus' club out of his hands, the banshee spun the diminutive man around and shoved him back toward his table. The leprechaun crashed into Dworkin and the pair were unceremoniously deposited into a chair with Fergus perched on the startled mage's lap.

"And stay there," she admonished, shaking a finger at them.

"But...but...," the leprechaun began.

Dagan glared across the room.

Fergus grabbed a bottle off the table and took a long swig of Irish courage. "This is the only place for two hundred miles that we can all get together without feeling like we are on display for the humans to leer at." The little man gestured around the bar, his voice rising. "You aren't seriously thinking about selling the place to them, *are you*?"

Dworkin dumped Fergus onto the floor. "That was *my* beer, you drunken gold-hoarder."

There was an ear-splitting screech from the corner. Marta, the scrying witch, pointed at the men in suits, shouting, "I can see it! They support the Humans First movement."

Morgan scowled at the men. "Humans First? The group that wants to create a registry of magical creatures?" She looked at Dagan. "Did you know about that?"

"Yeah," Dagan said sourly. "Just one of the reasons I turned 'em down."

Another witch from the coven that frequented the ORB offered up, "Please, let me turn them into toads!!"

Dagan shook his head. "No one is getting turned into toads today, Yvonne." He turned to the businessmen. "I've told you several times that my bar isn't for sale. Why are you here?"

Tab Harthan motioned to one of his aides. The tall assistant opened a briefcase, extracted a thin manila folder, and handed it to his boss.

The executive pulled a cream colored sheet from the folder and presented it to Dagan. "We realized that our initial offer was...insufficient. This place obviously has sentimental value that our appraiser failed to take into account. We'd like to remedy that oversight by raising our offer."

Dagan glanced at the sheet. His eyes bugged a little at the number of zeros it contained. Taking a deep breath, he started, "I appreciate...."

"Sir," the man interrupted, oozing charm, "we want to make you famous. Your specialty bock already has quite the local following, but you don't have the facilities to manufacture on the scale necessary to go global." Tab smiled and clapped Dagan on the back. "We do. So let's work together. Don't you want your brew famous worldwide?"

Dagan looked down at the paper and stroked his chin in consideration.

The bar erupted.

"Don't do it!"

"The money's not worth it!"

"Traitor!"

"They call *us* monsters," Isabella, the pixie, cried. "How can you even consider selling to *those* monsters." Her wings blurred, shedding deep red dust. "What next? Are *you* gonna join Humans First? Get your picture taken with the president."

Amid the uproar, Morgan pulled Dagan aside.

"I know the money would be nice, but...," she began.

Dagan shook his head. "Oh, it would be better than nice." He looked into her eyes, seeing the concern written there. "Do you know how much money I still owe? Do you have any idea how far into debt I went to open this place? Magical business licenses are expensive. I spend more for my insurance premiums every month than your and Kiz's paychecks *combined*. Humans in this state think magical creatures are a hazard, so they've made the rates astronomical, hoping we'll go somewhere else."

Morgan nodded in sympathy. "Yeah, NIMBY. Not In My Back Yard. I ran into the same thing when I went looking for an apartment. But still, if you need money so bad, couldn't you sell the recipe to someone who isn't backing the Humans First movement?" Dagan saw hope rising in her eyes.

He shook his head. "I wish I could. But," He shrugged his shoulders. "no one else has expressed interest. I suspect that those guys," He waved a hand toward the suits. "bought everyone else off."

She gave him a sour look. "And they say *we're* soulless."

Dagan bowed his head for a moment, lost in thought. Taking a deep breath, he looked up. *Maybe....*

"I've made my decision and," He looked around at his patrons and friends, hanging on his every word. "I don't think anyone here is going to like it."

Fergus shouted, "You can't sell them the bar! Or your recipe. People come here from all over."

"Shush, ya bloody leprechaun. It'll be all right."

Composing himself, he approached the bastard, Tab Harthan.

"Fine. I refuse to sell you the bar. But—I will sell you the recipe for my beer." He shook his finger at the suit. "Know this though, keep my name off of it. I refuse to be lynched by the magical community," He looked meaningfully at the gathered mob. "for selling it to you."

As if by magic, a contract appeared in the sallow man's hands.

Dagan gave it a cursory once over, then signed it.

The bar exploded in angry shouts.

Dagan ignored them.

The third member of the suit trio, a man with shoulders so broad he should have tipped over from their weight, stepped forward, opening a briefcase full of money for Dagan to inspect.

"Ok then," Dagan said, and snapped his fingers. A stained and yellowed scroll appeared in his hand.

Obviously taken aback at the casual display of magic, Tab snatched the scroll from him. Taking a quick glance at the recipe, he handed it to the tall man standing quietly behind him. When the aide nodded, the executive spun and marched out of the ORB, his flunkies close behind.

Turning to the still-protesting patrons, Dagan raised his

arms for silence.

Several minutes passed before the noise level dropped enough for him to be heard.

"All right, folks. Show's over." Pointing the the bar, Dagan added, "Drinks are on the house."

That got their attention.

Kiz and Morgan scurried back to work, quickly pouring drinks to mollify the assembled magical community.

Several hours later, Morgan stuck her head into Dagan's office, Kiz crowding in behind her.

"Got a moment, boss?"

"For you, Morgan, always," he said with a smile.

The banshee hesitated for a moment, then shook her head. "I don't understand. Why did you sell them the recipe? They'll make back what they paid you a thousand times over."

"Maybe," he said, cracking a grin, "but I doubt it."

Morgan gave him a sideways look. "Why? You gave them the recipe." She raised an eyebrow. "Unless that was a fake."

He shook his head. "Oh, no, it was the real thing. But it lists the main ingredient as nóinín."

Her brow wrinkled for a moment as she translated the old Gaelic word. "Daisies? Your beer is made from daisies? That should be easy for them to replicate."

Dagan chuckled.

"Is your Gaelic really that rusty, my dear? Try again."

Morgan's eyes lit up. "Oh! *Ancient* Irish daisies." She barked out a laugh. "That's hilarious."

"Sure enough, darlin'. If they use modern daisies, it'll taste horrible. They'll not be replicatin' *my* brew that easily."

Kiz shook his head, a confused frown on his red face. "Ancient daisies?"

Morgan smiled at the busboy, a wicked look on her pretty face. "Nóinín *are* Irish daisies, that's true. But you'd know them better by their modern name."

Dagan and Morgan shared a look, then spoke in unison.

"Dandelions."

SINKERS

Morgan set the tray down on the wooden table nearest the door.

"Here you go, boys, fugu sinkers for everyone. And the boss even added an air-breathing charm to this batch," She winked. "so you guys can stay on land tonight if you want." She shot a knowing look at the trio of wood nymphs in the far corner.

Ocessi reached eagerly for his to-go bag. "Tell Dagan that we really appreciate how much work he puts into making these pufferfish biscuits. We can't get them anywhere else."

"Well, there are advantages to having a pooka own the place. All the best chefs are pookas. Those celebrity chefs you see on TV? Every single one of them is a pooka. Well," she sighed, "except the few who are the descendants of Annapurna; they cheat!"

"Cheat?" The merman chuckled. "How?"

"When your mom is the Hindu goddess of food and nourishment and can produce unlimited meals, you learn a thing or two. So cooking is easy for them." She made a sour face. "That's cheating. They don't have to constantly *work* at their craft like Dagan does."

Acellant opened his bag and sniffed with delight. "Mm-mmm...smells just like mom used to make." Frowning, he asked, "Hey, what's with the new packaging, Morgan?"

The bartender huffed. "Last month, some wood nymphs picketed the bar and buried our front door in trash with our logo on it. So the boss decided to make them happy *and* cut waste by going with fully recyclable cutlery, plates, and packaging."

Ocessi nodded. "Recyclable stuff is a good first step, but I wish more businesses would switch to biodegradable packaging." He shuddered. "I accidentally swam through the North Pacific Gyre once. It took me three weeks to get all the plastic out of my scales."

Acellant nodded. "I've heard stories...."

Loud voices erupted from the far corner of the bar.

"Sorry, boys, duty calls," Morgan tossed over her shoulder as she hurried to investigate.

Morgan rushed up to find a green, scaly-skinned, humanoid dragon ranting incoherently at an old elven woman.

Another dragon leaned in, slamming both of his fists down on to the elf's table. "We followed your stupid map to the letter. 'Twas nothing there but water! We spent two whole weeks circling the area trying to find that damned island!"

Morgan recognized the dragons making a ruckus. *Great! What's crawled up Rudhri's butt this week?* she thought, shaking her head. *Jekas and Sandos promised to keep him on a short leash after last time. It took me nine months to get rid of all the scorch marks.*

"You lied to us! There was never an island there, let alone a treasure, was there?" Rudhri roared at the old woman, the fury of his voice knocking several glasses off nearby tables.

The ancient elf coughed into her voluminous sleeve before answering. "I know the treasure was there," she said in a hoarse voice. "I hid it. A long time ago." She coughed again. "I'm old and poor. I needed the money and you lot seemed so determined to find a *real* treasure."

Morgan grabbed the dragon's arm, interrupting the argument. "What are you going on about this time, Rudhri?"

He glared at Morgan, waving his free hand toward the old elf. "Tiatha sold us a fake treasure map."

The old woman shouted, "It's not fake. I buried that treasure myself!"

Morgan scowled at the angry dragon. "If it's been a long time, maybe someone else found it first. How would she know?" She glanced at the woman for confirmation. "Right?"

"No, no, no!" Tiatha said, shaking her head violently, her white braids flailing about. "I put it where no one would ever find it. It was still there when I left the island. I checked!"

"Ooooookay," Morgan said, focusing on Rudhri again. "I think you need to back off."

The dragon's eyes narrowed, a snort of flame and smoke escaping his nostrils.

Attempting to defuse the impending fiery disaster, the other dragons interrupted their smouldering leader.

Jekas spoke first. "Maybe your coordinates were off. Do you remember anything else about the island?"

"What was it near?" Sandos added. "We can search online for it."

Morgan turned back to the aged elf. "They've got a point, you know. Mapmaking has improved significantly in the last few centuries. Maybe yours is off by a bit. What was the name of the island you buried the treasure on?"

"Atlantis," the ancient elf spit out. "I'm sure you've heard of it."

Morgan's eyebrows shoot up. "Atlantis? But...but that sank thousands of years ago."

Tiatha's face fell. "Really? I hadn't heard." She shrugged. "Well, I *did* tell them it was a really old map!"

LOST AND FOUND

The Lord of the Flies zoomed through the open door of the pub. As he buzzed his way across the room toward Morgan, he eavesdropped on the bar's patrons. *You never know when a tidbit of info will come in handy.*

Marta whispered to her coven mate, Alexis, "I heard Celeste has a new boyfriend, but she won't tell me who...."

A harpy, decked out in punk rock gear, screeched, "...and Dex sees midnight runners outside our apartment complex every night ." She cackled. "I've found him cowering under the bed every morning this week."

Her companion retorted, "Aw, come on, Eileen. You're so mean. Why don't you just explain to that senile satyr husband of yours that it's only the vampire marathon team out for a training run...."

Finally reaching his destination, Satan took up a position on the wall directly over Morgan's head.

"I can't believe the lunch rush we had today," the banshee moaned, wiping up several spills on the counter with the towel from her back pocket.

On the other side of the serving window, Dagan folded his arms and leaned against the opening, eyeing their few remaining customers.

Wrinkling his brow, he asked the bartender, "That guy in booth six? He reminds me of your old friend. You know, the little brat that used to follow you around everywhere, back in the old country?" When she didn't answer, he added, "The one that always called you..." He scrunched up his face for a moment. "Mavourneen! That's it."

"Wow, that was a really long time ago." She twisted around to inspect the booth's inhabitant. "Oh," she said, eyes widening in recognition. "You mean Flynn? Flynn O'Callaghan?"

Dagan snapped his fingers. "Yeah, that one, the pretty boy with the red hair. Whatever happened to him, anyway?"

Morgan's face clouded. "He came to the new world by a... different route. The fool sold himself into bondage as an indentured servant."

Satan, intent on Morgan, was nearly flattened when Kiz's long tongue slapped the wall mere inches from him.

Morgan ducked, yelping, "What's gotten into you, Kiz? You almost hit me!" Straightening, she threw her towel at him.

The taciturn akaname caught it and pointed at the wall. "Fly! Hate them!"

Satan, still in fly form, launched off the wall, taking up a new position in the shadow of the bar, out of the akaname's sight.

"Me, too, but watch your aim, mister!"

"Sorry," Kiz mumbled, handing the towel back to her.

"Anyway," Dagan said, picking up the thread of their conversation, "what happened to him?"

Morgan made a sour face. "I hunted him down. It was the first thing I did when I got to the New World." She shook her head. "He was in a really bad situation. His...master was mistreating him. I barely resisted the temptation to.... But Flynn...he wouldn't let me help. He said he signed the contract all fair and square and he only had five more years till he was free." Reaching over, she tossed the wet towel into the laundry bin. Pulling out a fresh one, she continued, "I almost did it anyway, but...." The banshee trailed off, apparently lost in her memories.

The pooka reached through from the kitchen, putting a dark

hand on her shoulder. "What *did* you do?"

Morgan shrugged helplessly. "What *could* I do? I left. I couldn't stand to watch him be treated like that and not do *something*."

"So what happened to him, after that?"

"I don't know. I lost track of him. When I went back five years later, they said they'd sold his contract to someone in the Carolinas." She sighed. "It's my biggest regret. I never found him. I wish I knew if he was okay."

A lone tear slipped down Morgan's cheek.

Satan saw movement at the end of the bar. Kiz had spotted him again.

The akaname's tongue lashed out.

The Satan fly burst into flames.

He heard howls of "Oooooow! Hot hot hot!" as he teleported away.

A new location coalesced around Satan as he deftly shifted from fly to human form.

He took in the small, ornate room. Six young men struggled under the weight of an enormous casket. The gathered mourners stood, waiting to file out behind them.

A young man in an expensively tailored suit watched them leave, his bright red mohawk in sharp contrast to his cream-colored attire.

"What the devil?" The young man narrowed his eyes. "Who are...?" Recognition played across his face and he rolled his eyes. "Oh. You. I remember you, demon. You used to pester my cousin, Morgan."

"I did no such thing!" Satan said, outrage tingeing his voice. "I was courting her. You were a child. You obviously didn't understand the nuances of courtship back then."

Flynn raised an eyebrow. "Really? That's not how *she* described your interactions. She said...."

Satan interrupted. "A-hem. Be that as it may. The reason for this visit is that Morgan desires to see you. She is concerned for your well-being." Satan contemplated the boy's clothing and hairstyle choices. "And judging by your appearance, I'd say she has every reason to be concerned."

"There is *nothing* wrong with how I look," Flynn countered. "Not everyone dresses like it's still the turn of the last century. Get with the times, demon." He took a deep breath. "Anyway, you said Morgan wanted to see me. Why now, after all these years?"

Satan shrugged. "I have no idea why she does most things. But she said she wanted to see you." He spread his hands wide, bowing. "So here I am, ready to take you to her."

Flynn closed his eyes and dropped his head. He took a deep breath and looked up at Satan. "Where is she?" The young man chuckled and got a goofy grin on his face. "Probably someplace exotic. She always wanted to live somewhere like India or China."

Satan barely contained his laughter. "Nope! She's in Kansas. In a small town. In the middle of nowhere."

"And she's *happy* there?" Flynn asked, his red eyebrows scaling his forehead.

"I know. Hard to believe, isn't it." Satan shrugged. "But she is. She works for Dagan. They run a pub for otherworlders there."

Flynn nodded. "Yeah, that sounds like her." He raised the teacup of whiskey he'd been holding and downed the last few drops. "When do we ...."

Satan watched the teacup, suddenly bereft of support, drop to the floor before he snapped his fingers and disappeared.

"...leave?" Flynn finished, as the pair materialized in the parking lot of the Other Realms Brewpub.

The mohawked man yelped in surprise. "How'd...?"

Satan raised one eyebrow. "You do know who I am, right?"

"How could I forget, O Foul One? You make sure *everyone* knows who you are," he replied dryly.

"Now, now. Flattery will get you everywhere." Satan motioned toward the door. "Now be a good little redcap and go inside. She'll be *thrilled* to see you."

Flynn took a single step, then paused. Looking over his shoulder, he asked, "Why are *you* doing a good deed? What's in it for you?"

Satan narrowed his eyes. "Never you mind what's in it for me. This isn't about me, or you for that matter. This is about *her*." He pointed toward the bar.

Flynn raised his hands in surrender. "Okay. She's gonna be so surprised when I tell her who brought me here."

Satan's voice rolled like thunder. "NO! Don't you *dare* tell her that I had anything to do with this. Let her think *you* tracked her down." He let his true visage slip through. "If you tell her, I will make you wish you weren't immortal. You'll think Sisyphus got off easy."

Flames erupted around Satan as he shifted from human back into fly form.

Shaking his head, Flynn walked toward the door muttering, "Right. Don't mention the handsome brute in a suit. Got it."

Satan tucked himself into the boy's mohawk, hitching a ride into the bar.

Once inside, Flynn quietly stepped behind Morgan as the banshee wiped down one of the tables near the entrance.

"Hey there, Mavourneen."

The banshee gave a startled shriek.

Several patrons at nearby tables collapsed.

Satan, capitalizing on the distraction, teleported to a secluded table where he could watch the action, unobserved, in his human form.

"Oh, crap. Sorry, everyone," Morgan blurted out as she, Dagan, and Kiz raced to check on their patrons.

After determining that no one had died, Morgan returned to Flynn, anger bringing out her fierce beauty. "You know better than to startle a banshee! I could have killed someone."

Realization dawned on her face. "Wait. How'd you find me? I haven't seen you in over three hundred years."

"Just lucky, I guess." Flynn threw his arms around her. "But it *is* nice to see you again, cousin."

Morgan returned the hug. "Agreed. I've missed you, dearg caipín." She pushed back to look him in the eyes. "So, really, how *did* you find me?"

Satan made eye contact with Flynn from across the room and shook his head ever so slightly.

Flynn shrugged. "Beats the Hell out of me."

NIGHTMARES FOR RENT

Morgan unlocked and opened the door to her little house, tucked away at the end of a cul-de-sac.

"Love the green door," Flynn observed, following her inside.

She flipped on the lights and gave him a brilliant smile. "I know, right? It makes me think of home." Dropping her keys in a large wooden tray, she asked, "Knowing you, I'll bet your door is as red as your hair. Wherever it is you call home these days."

"San Francisco. And a' course it is. What other color would a bloody Red Cap's door be?"

"SF?" the banshee laughed. "I should have known. Lots of pretty boys there."

Morgan watched Flynn out of the corner of her eye as he roamed about her living room. She opened a bottle and poured two glasses of a nice Cynthiana red wine while her cousin perused her bookcase. She saw him linger on the array of pictures above her fireplace.

Morgan handed him the glass with Bugler's Vineyard's logo emblazoned across it. He pointed a long elegant finger at the framed pictures.

"Are they part of our family?" he asked, wrinkling his brow. "I thought I knew all our relatives."

"No, that's my family of choice. You know, people who come

into your life and then stay forever?" She made a face. "Unlike your birth family, who you can't get away from fast enough...," She trailed off, thinking back to the arguments she'd had with her mother when she moved to the new world. "or far enough, either, for that matter."

"Ah, I see." He looked pensive for a moment. "I haven't found many of those. Maybe a few, now that you've given a name to the concept."

To change the subject, she waved a hand around the room. "So, do you like my place?"

He nodded. "It's very nice. And very you."

She gestured toward one end of her massive leather sofa and took up residence at the opposite end. Settling in, she took a sip of her wine. "But, it was a long, hard road getting here."

Flynn joined her on the couch, asking, "Why? I'd've thought you'd have a lot of money saved up over the centuries."

Her face clouded. "Yeah, you'd think so. But between paying rent to my aunties for centuries, and the archaic attitudes around here about *our* kind of people, I went through a lot more of my savings than you might think."

Her mind flashed back to the first time she'd gone apartment hunting. "I finally put my foot down and told my Mom I was old enough to get my own place. It was right after I turned five hundred," She squinted one eye as she did the math in her head. "so...sometime in the late 1990s."

* * *

Morgan pulled her beat-up old Volkswagen Bug into the parking lot of the apartment complex, Johnny Hates Jazz's "Shattered Dreams" blaring from the radio.

"That song was number one on the charts ten years ago this week," the announcer said as the song finished up. "Coming up next...."

Morgan threw the car into park and killed the engine.

Taking a deep breath, she stared at the FOR RENT sign in the manager's window muttering to herself, "You can *do* this! You've lived with Auntie Badb for over two hundred years. It's about time you got a place of your own."

The manager, a motherly woman with bleached blond hair, first showed her one that Morgan thought was 'way too big,' then she showed her one that was 'smaller than the closet in my childhood bedroom. Finally, the manager opened the door of an apartment that Morgan instantly knew was 'just right!'

Jeez, I feel like Little Red Riding Hood!

She spun around in the middle of the large open area containing the kitchen, dining, and living rooms.

"Oh, my Gods, this is perfect!" she almost squealed. "It's airy and there's room for all my stuff! Oh," she said, pausing uncertainly. "What about the neighbors? Will my stereo bother them?"

The manager chuckled. "No, deary. The last tenant was a musician. He had the place soundproofed."

Morgan grinned. *Could this be any better? I think I'm in love! And it's in a secluded corner of the complex. I shouldn't have to worry about any humans spying on me.*

Then she paused. "Um, and how much is the rent, Mrs. Buckram?"

When the woman named a figure well within her price range, Morgan blurted out, "I'll take it."

"You'll need to fill out an application and pay the twenty five dollar fee for the credit and background checks, but I think we can get through the formalities by the end of the day," the woman said with a smile. "You're lucky. The apartment only became available yesterday."

Morgan hastily filled out the forms the manager gave her and paid the fee. "So, when will I know if I got the place?" she asked, trying to contain the excitement in her voice.

Mrs. Buckram patted Morgan's fidgeting hands. "If you leave me your pager number," She pointed to the device clipped to Morgan's purse. "I'll call you as soon as I find out. It shouldn't take too long."

Morgan was practically dancing as she re-entered the manager's office two days later, but stopped when she saw Mrs. Buckram's face.

Glancing up from Morgan's paperwork, the woman said severely, "Your credit report was fine, but there seems to be an error with your background check."

Butterflies seemed to be ramming the walls of Morgan's stomach.

"Um, what seems to be the problem?"

The manager shook the fax she was holding. "Says here you're a...banshee." She frowned. "But you certainly don't look like one. You're beautiful. Banshee's are ugly old hags."

Morgan bit her tongue and took a deep breath before replying.

"Well, the classic folklore around banshees was written by people who wanted us dead. We aren't like that, not at all." Morgan smiled, trying desperately to make the smile go all the way to her eyes.

The woman cleared her throat, raking her gaze back over Morgan's application.

Staring directly into Morgan's eyes, the manager intentionally dropped her application under the desk. "Ooops."

The woman smiled unconvincingly. "I'm sorry, Miss O'Grady, but I can't seem to find your application...anywhere."

"What? But you had it in your hand. Just a second ago." Morgan pointed. "You dropped it under your desk."

Pursing her lips, the woman bent down, pretending to search behind her desk.

"I don't see anything down here." Her words hit Morgan like darts.

A paper shredder growled to life beneath the desk.

Mrs. Buckram sat up and gave her a saccharine smile. "I'm sorry, but a nice, *normal* couple just rented the last unit we have available. By law, I have to let you know that you are more than welcome to apply again some time in the," The woman's voice dropped to the point where Morgan had to strain to hear her. "distant," Returning to normal volume, the manager spat out the last word. "*future.*"

Morgan didn't even protest. She knew magical prejudice when she saw it. Choking back tears, the banshee exited the office.

Outside, she raised her face to the clouded sky. Keeping her back straight and her steps firm, she marched away, leaving her dreams of independence on the doorstep.

She muttered to herself, "Someday...."

* * *

Morgan wiped a stray tear from her eye. "I haven't talked about that in decades."

Flynn slid down the couch and hugged her tightly. "Wow, cuz, I didn't realize it was that bad here. It's very different on the west coast. Everybody just accepts you for who you are in San Francisco. Gay, straight, magical creature, monster, whatever."

"I've heard that, but neither Dagan nor I do well in cities. We both prefer being out here in the middle of nowhere."

Flynn nodded, "Yeah, I remember." He glanced at the clock on the wall. "Damn. I need to get going. I've got a...friend who found you and sent me here. They're bringing me home at midnight." Flynn chuckled. "You know how these Cinderella-type things work. I should probably go outside so I don't accidentally take part of your house with me." He rose and headed for the door.

"So soon?" Morgan asked, following him. Standing on tiptoes, she kissed him on the cheek. "It's been great to catch up. Don't wait three centuries next time." She opened her front door. "You're welcome here anytime. You know that, right?"

"I do, Mavourneen. Thanks." Flynn gave her a bear hug then started down the steps to the walk. "I'll be back. You can count on it. *Somebody* has to look out for you."

Morgan was halfway to the kitchen when she stopped. *Dammit! I forgot to get his cell number.*

Opening the door, she saw Flynn standing alone in the middle of the cul-de-sac. Just as she opened her mouth to call out to him, she heard him shout.

"Satan! I'm ready to go home now."

Flames erupted next to him.

"Did you have a good visit, redcap?" she heard Satan ask.

Flynn nodded. "Yes. Thank you for making it happen."

"You didn't tell her that I brought you here, did you?" Satan inquired sharply.

"No. You asked me to keep that to myself. I'm a man of my word."

Morgan could hear the smile in Satan's voice. "Good. Let's get you home then."

With a snap of his fingers, the pair disappeared in a flash of flame.

Morgan closed the door and leaned against it, the shock of what she'd witnessed percolating through her body.

He found Flynn and brought him to me? Why would he do that?

Oh, my Gods, she gasped, burying her face in her hands. *He's serious.*

Satan really does *want to date me!*

LOVE IS IN THE AIR

"Where'd the roses come from?" Celeste asked, inhaling deeply.

Morgan made a face. "Satan."

The witch paled. "Satan? Please tell me you're kidding."

"Nope. He's been courting me off and on for *over five centuries!*" She shook her head. "And ever since I kicked his ass in a friendly game a few months ago, he's been sending me little 'gifts'." Morgan wrapped the last word in air quotes.

Shaking her head, Celeste leaned closer and hissed, "Well, at least *you* got flowers." She threw her hands in the air. "You see what I got? A big, fat, nothing."

"Gods," Morgan shouted. She slid the offending bouquet out of her sight. "I'll never understand human customs. Why give someone you're interested in dead flowers? Are you telling them you want them to die? It makes no sense."

Celeste cackled. "Honey, you should see what other cultures do. Kiz once left me a pile of his favorite things to lick." She shuddered. "Gods, the stench! It set up camp in my nostrils and refused to leave. Took two weeks before I could smell anything else."

"Ewww. I'm glad Kiz isn't interested in me like that." Morgan glanced at the card in her hand. "But Satan? Really? He's implied he wanted to date me for years, but now he's actually gone

48

and asked me out!" She sighed heavily. "And for Valentine's Day, no less." She put her elbows on the bar and buried her face in her hands. "I hate all this sappy crap. It's a made-up holiday. Just another excuse to sell chocolates and greeting cards to sentimental saps."

"Awww, c'mon, Morgan, you can't be *that* cynical," Celeste said with a laugh.

"Oh, yes, I can," Morgan said, grabbing her bar towel and wiping up an imaginary spill. "I'm a banshee, it's part of who we are. I'd rather have a night where I have to break up five or six fights than watch everyone sitting around being all lovey-dovey." She glared around the room. "Or worse, moping because they couldn't find a date."

"Well, I happen to love Valentine's Day," Celeste proclaimed. "I make a killing selling love potion espressos at The Magic Bean. Those folks at Starbucks can't compete with that!"

Morgan arched an eyebrow at her. "Only you would find a way to make money off of other people's suffering, Celeste. And you say *I'm* cynical."

Celeste shrugged. "It's a living." She snickered and pointed across the room. "It looks like some people are getting a head start on the holiday."

Morgan tracked where Celeste was pointing.

"NO! I do not need to see centaurs having sex in the middle of the bar, dammit!" She rolled her eyes. "Why did Kizumono have to take tonight off?"

Hurrying around the bar, she strode up to the centaurs' table.

"Helga, Hurley, get a room. I'm not against public nudity, but public sex? That's where I have to draw the line!"

Annoyed, the pair clomped toward the door.

"Humpf," Morgan huffed. "Didn't even leave me a tip."

She'd barely made it halfway back to Celeste when she saw another couple disrobing in one of the back booths.

Stalking over to them, Morgan slammed her fist down on the table.

"No sex in the bar! How many times do I have to tell you people? I know it's almost Valentine's Day, but give it a rest. There's a motel just down the block."

The vampire and the cherub both straightened, bewilderment on their faces.

"Sorry, Morgan. I don't know what came over us," offered Cherubiel, wiping blood off his neck. "We'll behave."

Damien retracted his fangs and nodded. "We just got carried away in the moment."

Back behind the bar, she chastised Celeste. "If you're going to sell love potions in here, you could at least encourage them to leave before they make a public spectacle."

"Nuh-uh. Don't blame me." Celeste shook her head forcefully. "I had *nothing* to do with it. Neither of those couples are clients of mine."

Morgan gestured furiously toward the dark tables in the back. "Then why did they practically have sex in one of my booths? There has to be a logical reason."

They both turned at the sound of the door chimes.

When Morgan saw how entwined the two gnomes were, she swore.

"Sheesh! What is it tonight? Is there something in the air?

Celeste scrunched up her eyes. "Hmmm, you might be onto something there." She waved her hands and muttered a quick incantation.

"Well...?" Morgan prompted after several minutes of silence.

Scanning the room, Celeste said, "Hummm, will you look at that." She pointed to a cloud of red-tinged energy which permeated the bar. "You were right. Something is up."

"I'll get to the bottom of this," Morgan said, following the darker strands of miasma toward the door.

The cold night air slapped her in the face as she left the building.

Dark energy swirled across the parking lot, terminating in a low-slung luxury vehicle.

It was bouncing wildly.

"Squeeek-squeeek-squeeek!"

Exasperated, Morgan rapped her knuckles on the driver's side rear window.

The fogged-over window slowly slid halfway down.

Inside, Morgan counted at least five bodies in various stages of undress.

"You need to move along. Whatever you are doing out here is bleeding over to everyone inside." She jerked a thumb towards the bar.

A woman, all alabaster skin and raven hair, blinked out at her.

"What do you have against a little passion in the parking lot?" A sly smile teased across her perfect lips. "Or are you just jealous you weren't invited?"

Eyes narrowing, Mogan threatened, "Leave willingly or I'll *make* you leave."

"Hah! It's a free country, you can't make us leave," the woman purred.

Morgan casually backhanded the driver's side mirror, sending pieces of plastic and glass skittering across the blacktop.

The woman's eyes flashed red. "You can't do that! Do you have any idea how much it's going to cost to replace that?"

"Don't know, don't care. You're upsetting my patrons, succubus. If you don't stop what you're doing right now, you'll be next."

"Fine!" the woman spat, straightening up her clothes.

Satisfied, Morgan strutted away. Moments later, she heard the engine roar to life and the car peel out of the parking lot.

Back inside, she grabbed a stout ale and downed it in one gulp. Wiping her mouth, she glanced at Celeste, muttering, "What a night! Hopefully that's the last…."

The door chimed again.

In the doorway stood the most beautiful man she'd ever seen. Long blond hair, piercing blue eyes, alabaster skin, and from what she could see though his tight clothing, a rockin' body.

The incubus crooked his finger at her.

"Come with me, my darling. Let's have a night that neither of us will *ever* forget."

She took a slight step forward. A hand flashed in front of her face and fingers snapped a bare inch from her nose.

Morgan's eyes followed the hand down the arm, down to a very concerned looking Celeste.

"Honey, I make love potions. I recognize love magic when I see it. And you've been hit, girl." She glanced at the man in the doorway. "Hard!"

"I don't care." Morgan said breathlessly. "I have to have him."

Celeste shrugged her shoulders, then cackled, "He's a luxury you can't afford, but it's your funeral, hon."

The sexy demon smiled as Morgan approached.

He led her outside to the same car she'd recently chased off. Opening the rear door, he ushered her inside.

The raven-haired succubus she'd confronted earlier sprawled in the back seat, a self-satisfied smile upon her lips.

"Looks like your threats are empty, barkeep. It's your turn to be frightened of *me*."

Morgan smirked. "Nope. You should still be scared of me. Love spells don't work on *demigods*."

"You can't be demigod! You look so...normal," the incubus exclaimed.

"I'm a daughter of the Morrigan. *And* I'm a banshee. My screams can kill."

Morgan opened her mouth.

And wailed.

A SLIP OF THE TONGUE

"Good eveni…" The maître d' of The Imperial raised his head, then sputtered to a stop as he caught sight of Kizumono.

Celeste giggled. *I bet they've never seen an akaname before. Even with all the magical creatures running around Kansas City, it's not often you see a six-foot-tall Japanese filth demon that looks like a red, warty caveman, especially one in a three-piece suit.*

The maître d' glanced over his shoulder repeatedly as he escorted them to a cozy table near musicians who were quietly warming up.

"And here's your table…uhhh, sir? Your server will be right with you." Once they were seated, the man vanished so quickly, Celeste suspected he had teleported away.

She glanced at the tall leather-bound menu briefly, before peering over it at Kiz.

"I can't wait to hear the music tonight. They're my favorite jazz trio."

The akaname looked up sharply. "You here before? With someone else?"

She smiled wickedly at him. "Of course. Do you think you're the first guy I've ever dated? I'm a witch, not some repressed mortal woman."

He let out a yelp, then ducked back down behind his menu.

Celeste snickered at her date's discomfort. *He's so easily embarrassed. For a filth demon, he so...pure.*

Soon enough, the waiter arrived.

The witch placed her order. "And for starters, I'll have a small wedge salad." She flashed a dimpled grin at the waiter. "After all, a girl's gotta watch her figure."

Kiz growled. "Kuso!" he swore in Japanese. "Me like *you*. Figure no matter."

The waiter cleared his throat. "And for you?" He shot a furtive glance at Kiz and hastily added, "Sir?"

"Steak."

"Which one, sir? We have several fine steaks available."

Kiz pointed at his menu. The waiter leaned in to read it.

Celeste chuckled under her breath. *That poor boy is about to shake himself apart. Kiz wouldn't hurt a fly.* A sudden memory popped into her head. *Oh, wait, there was that time that Winifred told me about.... Whatever! The waiter doesn't have anything to worry about.*

"Yes, s-sir. Number eleven, the 16 oz. T-bone steak with brandy peppercorn cream sauce. And for your sides?"

Kiz stabbed his finger toward the bottom of the menu this time.

"Ah, yes, the twice-baked potato, and...?"

"Cheese," the akaname grunted.

"Cheese?" The waiter looked confused for a moment, then nodded. "Oh! The gruyère mac and cheese. An excellent choice, sir."

"Oh, wait," Celeste said, snatching a small menu out of the waiter's hands as he turned toward the kitchen, "we'd like some wine." She leaned forward, giving Kiz a good view down her low-cut blouse, asking sweetly, "Would a bottle of 2013 Lang Reed Cab Franc be okay with you?"

The akaname bobbed his head. "Yes, yes, yes." The waiter nodded briskly and hurried toward the kitchen.

Soon, she was swaying to the quiet, familiar strains of Take Five, one of her favorite jazz pieces. *Hmmm, Kiz isn't much of a con-*

versationalist, but at least he doesn't go on and on about himself like most of my dates have. It's kinda nice to just be here, together, listening to the music.

She was jolted out of her reverie when the waiter slid a plate in front of her.

Celeste was still cutting her dinner into bite-sized pieces when she heard a soft noise and noticed that Kiz's plate was completely empty: meat, bone, and all.

Blinking, she blurted out, "Holy Hells, Kiz! That was fast."

The akaname shrugged. "Normal for me."

Shaking her head, she replied, "You know, there are these things called knives and forks." She waved her utensils at him with a bite of meat still impaled on her fork. "You could try using them. Maybe *savor* your meal instead of eating everything in one quick scoop of that ginormous tongue of yours."

He belched. "Food good. Still hungry." Looking longingly at her plate, he asked, "Taste?"

She hooked a protective arm between her plate and Kiz. "Nuh uh." She poked a thumb into her chest. "Mine."

Out of the corner of her eye, she caught sight of something moving near her elbow. Kiz's prehensile pink tongue had snuck up over the edge of the table and was inching toward her plate.

Ooh, sneaky. Maybe I should stab it with my fork? She contemplated that thought for a second before dismissing the idea. *Tempting, but no. That'd end our date way too early.*

She slapped the pink monster away from her plate.

"No means no!!"

Kiz's tongue snapped back into his mouth with an odd slurping sound. Celeste quickly covered her mouth, trying to hide the smile that spread across her face.

"Sorry," Kiz said forlornly. "Look good. Never have before."

Celeste shot him a wicked grin. "If you really want to eat something of mine that you've never had before, I've got some suggestions for what we can do *after* dinner."

She winked at him.

Kiz's eyes widened and his bright red face shifted to a

deep crimson. He hunched his shoulders and glanced around nervously. Leaning toward her, he whispered, "Later. Yes. Right." He shook his head. "Not now. Too public."

Celeste smiled to herself. *Aw, I embarrassed him. How adorable! Oh, if he blushes at the mere suggestion of sex, this is going to be a fun night!*

"And here are your desserts," the waiter said as he placed the confections on the table in front of them.

This smells heavenly! Celeste thought, picking up her fork and preparing to take a bite of the exquisite looking cinnamon pear tart.

"And I'll just leave this here with you." The waiter deposited a leather-bound folder on the table. "You can pay whenever you're...."

Kiz's tongue shot out, sweeping across his entire side of the table. In an instant, his dessert, the salt and pepper shakers, one of the lit candles...and the check, disappeared.

Burying her face in her hands, Celeste couldn't help but chuckle. *Oh dear Gods, he even managed to lick that poor man's hand.*

The waiter let out a high-pitched scream and fled.

Every eye in the room turned towards them. Even the jazz trio paused.

Kiz squeaked out, "Ooops. Nervous."

After a few beats, the music resumed.

Celeste shook her head. "Well, I *was* going to pay, but I guess you are now."

"Fine, I pay." He scowled. "But, why?"

The witch smirked. "You ate the check, that's why. And I'm certainly not going after it *now*."

The akaname pouted. "Sorry. Accident."

Celeste nodded. "Ah, a slip of the tongue, you might say."

Kiz scowled at her. "Ha ha. You funny."

She placed her hand over his on the table. "Aww. Can you forgive an old witch for her silly sense of humor?"

"Not old. Sexy." He covered their joined hands and squeezed

gently.

"I'll show you just how sexy I can be, you warty beast," she said, her voice going husky, "once we pay the check and get out of here.

Kiz's eyes lit up. Raising his hand, he shouted over the music, "Waiter. New check. Now!"

THE DATE FROM HELL

"Damn, girl, you look fine," Celeste cackled. "Why are you all dressed up in the middle of the day?"

"You like it?" Morgan asked the witch sitting at the bar, twirling around, the dangling leather lacings of the belt and deeply-slit black skirt flaring out, revealing her thigh-high, laced boots. The stiletto heels added four inches to her stature. "It's for my...," Her voice dropped to a whisper. "date."

The witch's face was a mask of horror. "You're seriously going out with Satan? Are you crazy, girl?"

Morgan winced, hastily clamping her hand over the other woman's mouth. "Shhhh! Not everyone in the bar needs to know that." She shrugged one shoulder. "I kinda felt like I should at least give him a chance."

Celeste looked down her nose at Morgan's hand until the banshee removed it.

"It was the flowers, wasn't it?"

"Well, that *and* a favor he did for me recently." She plopped down onto the bar stool next to her friend. "Besides, he grows on you after a while."

Celeste snickered. "Like a fungus?"

Morgan made a face at the witch. "It's been a long time since I've been out on a date." She took a deep breath. "My mother is very...protective. And violent! At least he's not scared of her."

Celeste nodded. "That's understandable." The witch's eyes lit up as she spotted something across the room. "Well, good luck. I'm off. *I* have a date tonight too."

Morgan couldn't keep the surprise out of her voice. "Oh? Weren't you just complaining last night that you didn't get flowers for Valentine's Day?"

Celeste smiled wickedly. "Just because I didn't get flowers *doesn't* mean a girl can't have a good time."

"Hey, Kiz," Morgan said, as the akaname joined them. "What are you doing here? Your shift was over a couple hours ago. "

Kiz pointed at Celeste. "Date night. Movies. Sex." He wrapped his arms around the witch.

"Wait! What?" Morgan gasped.

"The boy may not be a stunning conversationalist," Celeste confessed, "but he's sweet and kind and thoughtful. Besides, have you *seen* his tongue? Girl, let me tell you, the last few weeks have been heavenly."

"TMI! Too much information. Overshare!" Morgan cried, scrunching up her eyes and frantically waving her hands, trying to chase away the mental image the witch conjured.

"Anyway," Celeste said, laughing off Morgan's reaction, "where are *you* going? That's the fanciest outfit I've ever seen you in."

"Hmmph," she grumbled. "He wouldn't tell me. He said he wanted to surprise me and I should wear something fancy." She raised an eyebrow at Celeste. "Think this'll suffice?"

A much deeper voice replied, "Oh, it most certainly will."

Satan stood just inside the ORB's glass doors, his wide eyes appraising Morgan from her tousled red hair to the toes of her laced boots.

Celeste stood, grabbing her coat from the back of the barstool. "And...that's our cue. C'mon, Kizzy, we've got a busy night ahead of us."

Morgan watched the pair carefully avoid Satan as they headed for the exit.

That's when she noticed a child standing next to Satan.

She frowned. "And who is this?"

"Oh," he said, smiling down at the girl, "this is my daughter, Lucy."

"And this is Beelz," the child offered, holding a doll up for Morgan's inspection. The stuffed animal had yellow stripes, two horns, and a huge medallion around its neck.

"Riiiiight. Beelz." Morgan had never felt comfortable around children. They were just too...unpredictable. *Hell*, she thought, *like* Satan *is predictable!*

Deadpan, she sniped, "I don't date men with children."

"Lucky for you then," He flashed her a sexy grin. "I'm not a man. I'm an angel."

Morgan fired back sardonically, "Sure you are. And I'm the President of the United States."

"Are you serious? They couldn't manage to elect a perfectly qualified *human* woman. They'd never vote for a non-human one," Satan offered. "Besides, Lucy is just visiting. She lives with her mortal parents here on Earth."

Chuckling, Morgan replied, "So she's your daughter? According to the movies, your only child is a boy named Damien."

"Hollywood!" He rolled his eyes. Leaning over, he kissed Lucy on the forehead. "Time for you to go home, sweetie." Satan snapped his fingers and the little girl vanished.

A sly smile spread across the devil's handsome face. He helped Morgan into her jacket then held out his hand. "Shall we?"

"Um, sure," she replied.

The air changed. Day became night.

Morgan turned her head, taking in the structure above them. She let out a startled squeak.

"The Eiffel Tower? Paris?"

Satan bowed, kissing the hand he still held.

"Of course," he purred. "I wanted our first date to be special. Could anything be more special than dinner at Le Jules Verne at the Eiffel Tower?"

Morgan gulped. "I suppose...."

They took a private elevator to the second floor. They'd scarcely stepped off when the maître d' hurried over, his tuxedo tails flapping in his wake.

"Bienvenue, Mr. Morningstar. Your usual table is ready. Please follow me."

Morgan raised an eyebrow at that. "Usual table, huh?"

"Of course," Satan said, taking her elbow as they made their way to their table. "I helped finance this place. The least they could do was guarantee me a table whenever I want one."

Morgan looked at him sideways as they took their seats. "Bring a lot of dates here, do you?" She glanced out the windows. "I bet this view impresses the multitudes of women…" She squinted at him. "*and* men you've brought here over the years."

Satan paused as the sommelier rushed up to their table and poured champagne for him to taste. After he'd taken a sip and nodded, the wine steward filled both their glasses and hurried away.

"I'll have you know," he said archly, "that I haven't been on what *you* would consider a 'date'," he made air quotes around the word, "since I met you, my dear."

Morgan raised a single eyebrow. "Riiiight. *You've* been celibate for five centuries?" She shook her head. "I'm not buying that for a second."

Satan chuckled. "Oh, I never said anything about being celibate. I said I haven't gone on what *you* would consider a date."

She thought about that for a moment. "Ok, fine. What do *you* consider a date then?"

If anything, his grin got wider as he leaned across the table toward her. "Why, wine, dinner, and dancing. That sort of thing. Courtship." He paused to take another sip from his champagne flute. "Sex is easy. Relationships are hard."

Morgan tipped her glass toward Satan and then took a drink. "Too true."

Her phone rang.

Glancing at the caller ID, she muttered, "Great. Just great." She squeezed her eyes shut. "It's my mother."

Satan rolled his eyes, obviously remembering the last time he'd encountered the Goddess Macha.

Morgan sighed deeply and swiped her finger across the phone.

"Hi, mom. No, mom. Yes, mom. Yes, I'm on a date." She put a hand across her eyes. "No, I'm perfectly fine. No, you don't have anything to worry about. I *can* take care of myself." She pulled the phone away from her ear at the sound of Macha's screeching. Morgan screamed back, "Mooooom!" The diners at the next table shot a dirty look at her.

I am going to kill Flynn for telling her about my date!

When the yelling had stopped and she thought it safe to put the phone back up to her ear, Morgan began, "Yes, mom, I am on a date with Satan. Yes, I know what you think of him. He's really not *that* bad...."

Satan cocked his head at that. He raised a finger at Morgan and began to speak, "I...."

Poof.

Macha herself stood beside their table. Several diners let out startled squeaks and squawks.

Glaring at Satan, the Goddess growled, "I thought I told you to leave my daughter alone, Old Scratch."

Satan held up both hands in surrender. "I have not coerced her in any way. I have simply wooed her." He pushed his chair back and stood, his usual smile gone. "If I'd wanted to force this relationship, I would have done so centuries ago rather than dragging it out this long." He turned to Morgan, a slight twinkle in his eyes. "Not that I would *ever* try to force you into anything, my dear."

Morgan's mother shook her head, fury written large across her fair face. "I don't care what either of you want. I'm telling you that this date is over." When Morgan tried to object, Macha slashed a hand through the air. "OVER!"

The war goddess reached for her.

Jerking away, Morgan crossed her arms. "No, mother!"

"He's a demon! You can't marry a demon."

"Whoooa!" Morgan and Satan said in unison, their eyes

widening.

Morgan continued, "Who said anything about marriage? This is just a simple date. A *first* date, at that."

Satan added, "Besides, I'm not a demon." He pressed a hand to his breast. "*I* am an *angel*."

Trying not to laugh, Morgan deadpanned, "A fallen one."

Adjusting his suit jacket, Satan said smugly, "Still an angel."

"Aargh!" Macha cried, making another grab for Morgan and succeeding this time. "I will not let this happen. *My* daughter will not date Satan." Her whole body thrummed with outrage. "We're leaving. Now. There isn't any place on this Earth that you can hide from me."

Satan blinked. "Oh, Macha, you are so right. There isn't any place on this *Earth* where we could hide." Taking a deep breath, he snapped his fingers.

Instead of the simple shift of location of their last transport, the three of them were engulfed in flames. When the fire receded, Morgan found they were standing on an open plain, large bonfires burning off in the distance.

Satan swept his hands in an arch. An exact replica of Le Jules Verne materialized around them.

From the shadows, a hulking demon dressed as a waiter stalked towards them. In his huge, taloned hands he carried a tiny notepad and pencil.

"Hiya, Boss," the beast said in a gravelly voice that would have been appropriate for a creature made of boulders. "What can I get you tonight?"

"We'll have two specials, Belphegor." Satan pointed at Macha. "After you escort our...uninvited guest to the door."

Macha's eyes blazed. "I'm not done...."

Satan focused his full attention on the Goddess.

Deadly serious now, he said, "*You* were the one who said 'no place on Earth' was safe from you. Well, this is *my* realm. You have no power over either of us here. Now, leave so we can go back to enjoying our date." He shooed her away.

Macha took a step toward them, murder on her face.

"Just remember," he said sweetly, "I only ask nicely the *first* time."

Satan flipped his hand in Macha's direction.

The war goddess vanished.

Satan calmly pulled out a chair for Morgan, then took his own seat.

Looking around nervously, Morgan asked, "Um, where did you send my mother?"

"Oh, don't worry," Satan said dismissively. "I didn't hurt her. I just sent her back home."

While Morgan tried to decide where exactly he might consider Macha's home, Belphegor appeared at their table, a bottle of wine clasped in his scaly, red hands.

"Here ya go, boss. A nice Château Margaux Balthazar 2009."

The demon poured a glass for each of them, waiting only long enough for his master's approval.

"Excellent," Satan said, nodding like a king to his subject.

Looking at Morgan over the rim of his wine glass, he said, "I'm terribly sorry that the view isn't as good here as it was on the Eiffel Tower." He gave her a wry smile. "At least we won't be interrupted now."

She took a sip of the wine and raised her eyebrows. "Oh, this is heavenly!" Realizing what she'd just said, Morgan laughed. "You know what I mean."

The twinkle in his eyes told Morgan he was enjoying their conversation.

"Yes, it is divine, isn't it." Tilting his head, he continued, "But anyplace you are would qualify for that appellation, in my view."

The only thing Morgan could think to do was roll her eyes. "Flattery, sir, will get you nowhere."

He gestured toward her with an open hand. "But it's not flattery on my part. It's a sincerely held belief."

Morgan felt her cheeks warm, though a shiver ran down her spine.

"Uh huh. Sure."

"You wound me, my dear, by not believing me."

At that moment, their dinner arrived, consuming all of their attention with its fine presentation, exotic flavors, and mouth-watering aromas.

The ting of Morgan's fork on her dessert plate made Satan look up from his own sugary concoction.

"That was incredible," Morgan pronounced. "I can't believe the underworld has food like this."

The Master of Hell laughed.

"Well, of course we do. What do you think we use to torture people with?" He raised his eyebrows at her questioning look. "The smells from this kitchen waft over the section of Hell reserved for the sin of gluttony." His grin could truly be called wicked. "They get to smell but never taste."

Morgan nodded. "Impressive."

"I'm so glad you appreciate my handiwork. Torture, like anything else, is an art." He folded his napkin and laid it across his empty plate. "I've worked very hard to perfect my techniques."

Morgan glanced down at her watch.

"I'm having a great time, but it's getting late and I do have to open the bar tomorrow morning." She looked up at Satan. "Could I get a lift home?"

"Why, of course, dear lady." He stood, rounded the table, and helped Morgan into her jacket. Taking her hand, he snapped his fingers.

Instantly Morgan found herself standing outside her house, within the yellow circle of its porch light.

"Thank you for one Hell of a night." She smiled at the play on words, then turned to unlock her door.

He cleared his throat, making her look back at him.

"I have one question for you...." He cast his eyes down and shuffled his feet. "I thought...I mean, you said you wouldn't date me 'in a thousand years,' but it's only been a few hundred." He stared into her eyes. "So what changed?"

A tiny smile fought to conquer her lips.

"I know what you did. With Flynn." Satan's eyebrows rose. "I saw you two together after he left my house the other night."

Satan had the decency to blush, a look Morgan never imagined seeing on him.

"I didn't want you to know that I had anything to do with that."

"I know," she said, touching him lightly on the arm.

"But...." Satan began.

She turned fully toward him, grabbed his lapels, and kissed him soundly.

"That's why," Morgan said over her shoulder as she opened her door. "You got time off for good behavior."

* * *

Authors' note: *This isn't the last you'll be hearing from Lucy.*

PILLS 'N' POTIONS

*This collection was originally going to be stories from our Modern Magical Universe, but the Other Realms Brewpub decided it wanted to be the star of the show. This left one of the other stories in this world sitting on the sidelines. We thought we'd throw it in as a bonus for our readers. Here's **Pills 'n' Potions**. Enjoy!*

* * *

"And I fear it's getting worse," Delta Riptide said, reaching for another fresh scone and slathering it with the boysenberry jam Opal had brought to their monthly tea. "First it was my knees." The witch rolled her eyes. "Have you ever tried to land a broomstick with bad knees? Ass over teakettle, three out of four times! I've had to replace my broom twice in the last six months." She took a bite and closed her eyes with pleasure. "I mean, I'm only three hundred and ten. I shouldn't be breaking down already."

"I know what you mean," Wendy Welkin replied. "Rainy weather bothers my shoulders and neck something fierce." She held up her hands to stop the retorts she knew were coming. "Yes, yes, I know I can influence the weather and keep the rain away, but sooner or later, the farmers get on my case." She looked around the table. "Do the rest of you have problems like this?"

Opal Clay, the earth witch, and Blaise Sparks, the fire witch and only male present, both nodded.

"My sciatica...." began Blaise.

"Migraines...." Opal said.

"No, no, I don't want to hear anymore about it," Delta said, scowling. "Even hearing about all of that makes me hurt." She shook her head. "Let's talk about something pleasant...like your kids."

That earned her a smile from Opal.

"Crystal got accepted at Elle Mental's Foundational School of Magic. She starts this fall." Her look of pride vanished as her shoulders sagged. "I'm really stressed about her going out on her own though." She shook her head sharply, causing her long brown hair to dance about her face. "That girl's so naive, I'm positive someone will take advantage of her. I mean, what'll happen when they find out she can bring raw diamonds and gems out of the earth whenever she wants?" She sighed. "And it's not like she keeps it a secret, either. She constantly shows off on her Instagram page!"

Wendy put a soothing hand on Opal's arm. "I know exactly how you feel. My son Storm may still be under my roof but he's getting wilder by the day. He absolutely loves showing off for the other boys that he can fly." She blushed furiously. "Last week I caught him and some boy—who I hope is his boyfriend—fooling around in the clouds over our house!"

Blaise shuddered. "Wasn't that kind of...wet? I know clouds look all light and fluffy, but they're made of water droplets, after all."

Opal sniggered. "Not everyone is guaranteed to have sex someplace warm and dry like you!"

"Now, now. Enough about people's sex lives." Delta said, blushing.

They all heard a loud noise from the sea witch's kitchen.

Delta continued, "That reminds me, I absolutely *must* introduce you to my new intern, Nicki. She's only been with me three weeks and she's already spellcasting and making potions."

"Really? I've never had an apprentice with that much talent," Blaise said, lighting a cigarette with a snap of his fingers.

Both Wendy and Opal, who'd lectured the fire witch about smoking for several decades, scowled at him.

He ignored them. As usual.

"I haven't either," Delta added. "You remember my last apprentice, Sue Nami? Her sophomore project flooded the Mississippi!" She poured herself another cup of tea, adding two heaping spoonfuls of sugar. "I shipped her back to her folks in Japan in a hurry, I can tell you."

"Well, I think it's about time that the younger generation takes the old ways seriously," Blaise said, exhaling a linked chain of smoke rings into the air.

"And here's my apprentice now," Delta said, as a dark young woman with black hair, several ear piercings, and a nose ring entered the room via the kitchen door.

"I brought you something," she said brightly, presenting a tray with four vials. "I thought you'd all like to sample my take on a pain relief potion."

Delta raised her eyebrows. "Pain relief potion? You aren't supposed to start that lesson for another month."

The girl beamed. "I read ahead when I heard you talking about your aches and pains earlier. I figured you could use a few pain-free days." She offered the vials to everyone at the table. "Tell me what you think, okay? I added a bit of mint and cinnamon to the recipe."

Blaise took a cautious sip. His eyebrows shot up. "This is amazing. Better than my mother's brew, even." He gave the young apprentice a conspiratorial look. "But don't tell her that."

Nicki laughed. "I promise."

The other three quickly tossed back their potions and began stretching.

Blaise exclaimed, "Ahhh, that's the first time in five years that my sciatica hasn't given me fits." Getting up, the old man took a few dancing steps. "Girl, you are a miracle worker."

Nicki blushed at the praise, her face reddening up to her hairline. The tattoos on her arms actually glowed for an instant or two.

The air witch, Wendy, currently floating around the room, asked, "So how did you get so good at potions and spellcasting at such a young age?"

The girl shrugged. "I guess it just comes naturally to me."

Opal sighed. "This feels so nice, but I wish it would last longer than a couple days."

"Oh, don't worry. I made extra that I'm condensing down into pills for you all to take home." She winked at Opal. "Us witches have to stick together, after all."

Giving them a little wave, she headed back to the kitchen. Behind her, Wendy landed gracefully on her chair and the senior witches resumed their tea party.

Just as Blaise began to speak, a blast of noise from the kitchen forced them all to cover their ears.

Shouting to make himself heard, Blaise demanded, "What's that horrible racket?"

"Nicki's music," Delta shouted back, squinting against the sound. "She says the music helps her raise energy for complex spells."

"I don't see how listening to *that*," Opal shouted, "could help you do anything except..." The music fell by a few decibels. "...lose your hearing," the earth witch finished at a normal volume.

Pouring herself another cup of tea, with honey this time, Delta explained, "She doesn't just listen to it. She writes songs too. She's been rhyming her whole life. That's why her spellcasting is so damn good." The sea witch winced at a particularly graphic chorus from the next room. Leaning in, she dropped her voice. "Personally, I can't stand the sound of it," She waved towards the other room. "but her talent speaks for itself."

Nicki re-emerged from the kitchen, bearing a large plate of chocolate chip cookies.

"Oh, thank you, dear. These smell heavenly," Wendy exclaimed, taking two of the still-warm treats.

"Well, I need to get back to my brews," Nicki said. "I have to prepare for my challenge tonight."

"Challenge?" Blaise asked, helping himself to a cookie.

"She does freestyle music battles," the sea witch replied, explaining, "That's where two people compete to create songs off the top of their heads. The audience decides the winner. And she's won. A lot."

The fire witch shook his head. "Wow. So that's what the world's coming to, eh? Spellcasting through rap music?"

Delta shrugged. "I don't care how the next generation works their magic if it means that I can feel this good."

Opal paused mid-chocolate-chip-cookie-bite. A lascivious look came over her face. All the assembled witches began hastily disrobing.

From the other side of the room, Nicki peeked through the kitchen door to see the four older witches engaged in a rather acrobatic sexual encounter.

"Guess the lust potion I added to those cookies worked." Nicki smiled, turning back to her simmering cauldrons. "Maybe next time they won't knock my music."

We hope you enjoyed the Other Realms Brewpub. If so, please help others find us by leaving a review at http://amazon.com/dp/B07W62L3BV/.

Visit our website, http://www.thirdwar.net/ to read more than 50 FREE short stories that we've written over the years. While you're there, sign up for our newsletter and you'll receive an exclusive short story not available anywhere else.

UNIDENTIFIED LOVE PREVIEW

Here's an excerpt from our first short story anthology, *Unidentified Love*. Follow Nick, a military brat who will one day head up the military's search for extraterrestrial life, and Ben, the boy he falls for who is secretly an ET.

"I didn't mean to fall for you, it just happened," I told him while we sat together in the bed of his truck under the crescent moon.

Nick looked at me, those big, brown eyes wet with unshed tears. "I can't. I like you, but..." His words tapered off as he looked down at his feet. He mumbled out some more words, but I couldn't hear him.

I wanted so desperately to reach out and touch him, comfort him somehow, but fear kept me on my side of the truck.

"I can't hear you when you mumble into your overalls like that. Look at me, please." *He's so upset he can't even look at me. I shouldn't have said anything. Just forget it. Let's go back to being friends. Please, please, please.*

"I said, 'Why did you have to tell me you liked me like that?' I'm not..." He paused, looking everywhere but at me. "I don't...."

"I know, you don't feel that way about me. Forget I said anything." My face was practically on fire with embarrassment.

"Ben, stop. Just stop!" Nick shouted.

Now *I* was the one close to tears.

Nick reached out and took my hand. "I do have feelings for you, but my dad.... He's a general at the base. He expects me to join the military and follow in his footsteps. I can't do that if I'm with you. They kick people like us out. My dad told me a story once about a guy they thought was gay in their platoon. They beat him up so bad that he wasn't able to walk ever again." He hopped out of the pickup and paced back and forth between the edge of the cornfield and his truck. "He *laughed* when he told me that story. He helped break a man's spine so he'd never walk again and he bragged about it, like it was one of those damn medals on his chest. What do you think he'd do to me – or to you, for that matter, if he found out. I can't take that kind of chance."

My hearts had been doing the Snoopy Happy Dance ever since Nick admitted that he had feelings for me too. I knew he was right, I should be worried about his father's reaction, but I couldn't think about that. All I could think about was that Nick liked me.

"Ben!" Nick snapped his fingers in front of my face. "Earth to Ben." He chuckled at me. "I swear, sometimes it's like your brain is in outer space."

I couldn't resist a laugh of my own. *If you only knew how true that was.* "You'd like that, wouldn't you. You've been fascinated by all things extraterrestrial ever since we saw ET when it came out a few months ago."

"Just you wait. One day, I'll prove that ETs are real." Nick placed his hand over his heart. "It's my destiny, I just know it."

"Maybe you're right. Maybe one day you will discover that ETs have been visiting Earth for a long time."

"Don't laugh at me. I'm going to do it," Nick said, puffing out his chest.

"I'm not laughing at you. It's one of the things that made me fall for you. I think it's cute."

Nick smiled up at me.

I jumped down beside my friend and pulled him into a hug. When I drew back, Nick had this strange look in his eyes.

"What?"

The only response I got was Nick dragging me deep into the head-height corn field.

Afterwards, we lay spent, lost in thought.

I broke the silence. "That was amazing. I thought it would be good, but, wow."

Nick smiled at me. "That was...incredible." But the smile faded and Nick's face turned grim. "Ben, this can't happen. It's nice to dream, but... It. Can. Never. Happen. Again. We can't be together like that."

"Maybe not now, but someday. Maybe someday things will change and we can be together," I offered.

Nick shook his head. "I don't think that will ever happen. If it does, well, then maybe...."

"If it does," I said, "then I'll be right here waiting for you."

The watch on Nick's wrist beeped. "Ah shit. Dad's going to be home soon. I have to go." He stood, hastily making his clothes presentable.

"Are you sure you can't stay just a little longer?" I asked. "We could...."

Nick shook his head. "I can't. If I'm not home when dad gets there, he'll get pissed and be shitty to me all evening."

I adjusted my clothes as we walked back to his truck.

The truck's engine roared to life.

Leaning through the open window, I couldn't resist giving him a kiss goodbye.

Several long moments passed before he broke the kiss. "I gotta go. I'm late already."

I smiled. "Ok, but if you change your mind, you know where to find me." I gestured with my head toward the farmhouse on the other side of the cornfield.

"I know. See you later, Ben," Nick shouted as his truck pulled away.

He was barely out of sight when *my* watch beeped.

I raised my wrist to my mouth. "Yes, Mother. You can beam me up now."

A soft glow surrounded me as I was transported to the waiting shuttle.

I'd just materialized when she started lecturing me. "You shouldn't get involved with a human," she said, stabbing a finger at me. "He's just going to break your hearts. You know how they are, humans are too fickle. They fall in and out of love whenever the wind changes direction. They don't mate for life like our people."

Ben sighed. "Nick's different, Mom. You'll see."

His mother shook her head and rolled her eyes.

Glancing at the monitor over her shoulder, I watched Nick's truck do an abrupt u-turn and start heading back to where we'd parted.

"Looks like you were wrong, Mom. Nick does love me. Beam me back down there."

If you like this short and want to read the rest of Ben and Nick's story, you can pick up *Unidentified Love* at http://amazon.com/dp/B01DOPS4G4/.

To read more short stories from Orion and Kyros and to receive advance notices of new releases, check out our blog at http://www.thirdwar.net/. While you're there, sign up for our newsletter and you'll receive an exclusive short story not available anywhere else. Don't worry, we don't like our email inboxes stuffed everyday so we won't flood yours either!

OTHER BOOKS BY ORION AND KYROS

Dreaming of Xeres

Do you feel like you don't belong here? Maybe you don't. Maybe you reincarnated from another planet. What would you do if one day you found out that your loved ones had once lived on another planet? That they lived entire lifetimes before reincarnating here? Dr. Riley MacPherson faces that dilemma when Tessa, his girlfriend, reveals in a past life regression that she's originally from another world. One with orange-colored trees with blue leaves. This sends him on a quest to uncover all he can about this other world, Xeres. Along the way, Riley discovers more people who remember lives on that other world, and some of them are dying. Can Riley uncover their shared past before an ancient enemy destroys their future?

Find it on Amazon at http://amazon.com/Dreaming-Xeres-Third-War-Book/dp/0996266518/

Unidentified Love

General Nick Pearson has been in love with Ben Smith since they were kids. Heading the military's search for extraterrestrial life from the fabled Area 51, he's unaware that the love of his life is one of the aliens he's spent his life searching for. Will Ben's secret tear them apart or can the star-crossed lovers live happily ever after?

Visit our website, http://www.thirdwar.net/ to read over 50 FREE short stories that we've written over the years. While you're there, sign up for our newsletter and you'll receive an exclusive short story not available anywhere else.

ABOUT THE AUTHORS

Orion grew up in the Midwest on a farm, where she enjoyed the company of cows, dogs, cats, chickens (not so much!), and, most of all, horses! If she had her way, *all* children would be raised on farms, tanned and barefooted! (She refuses to discuss the snow, tornadoes, and spiders.)

She began reading at an early age and never stopped (which has played havoc with her sleep). Once she retired from libraries, teaching and too many other occupations to mention, Orion started writing short stories, flash fiction, and novels, both alone and with her co-author Kyros Amphiptere.

She currently resides in western Washington State with her cats Missy and Oliver, her piano, and an ever-growing number of books, more than many libraries.

Kyros also grew up in the Midwest. Not far from where Orion grew up, actually. He began writing short stories soon after reading Madeleine L'Engle's Wrinkle in Time series in grade school.

He met Orion shortly after he moved to Seattle when he turned 21. They were friends, roommates, and even co-owners of a bookstore during the 18 years he lived there. But it wasn't until after he moved to California that they started seriously collaborating on writing. He had just lost his job and decided to finally sit down and write the novel that had been bouncing around in his head since the mid-90s.

He currently resides in the San Francisco Bay Area with his two husbands, two dogs, and a very opinionated African Grey parrot named Abby.